KU-300-279

This Book
Belongs To:

Kipper

Story Collection

KIPPER

KIPPER'S TOYBOX

KIPPER'S BIRTHDAY

KIPPER'S SNOWY DAY

A division of Hodder Headline plc

Kipper

Mick Inkpen

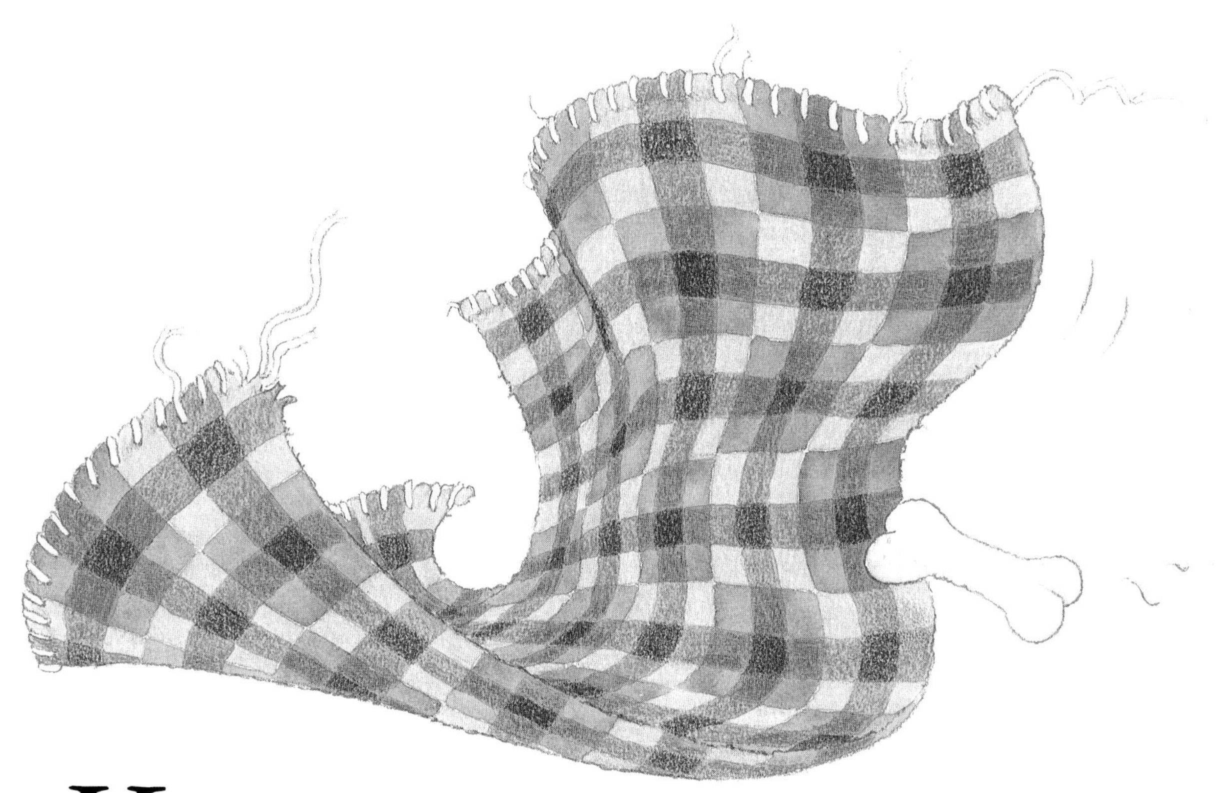

Kipper was in the mood for tidying his basket.

'You are falling apart!' he said to his rabbit.

'You are chewed and you are soggy!' he said to his ball and his bone.

'And you are DISGUSTING!' he said to his smelly old blanket.

Out they went.
'That's better!' said Kipper.

But it was not better. Now his basket was uncomfortable.

He twisted and he turned. He wiggled and he wriggled. But it was no good. He could not get comfortable.

'Silly basket!' said Kipper…

…and went outside.

Outside there were two ducks. They looked very comfortable standing on one leg.

'That's what I should do!' said Kipper. But he wasn't very good. He could only...

…wobble.

Some wrens had made a nest inside a flowerpot. It looked very cosy.

'I should sleep in one of those!' said Kipper. But Kipper would not fit inside a flowerpot.

He was much too big!

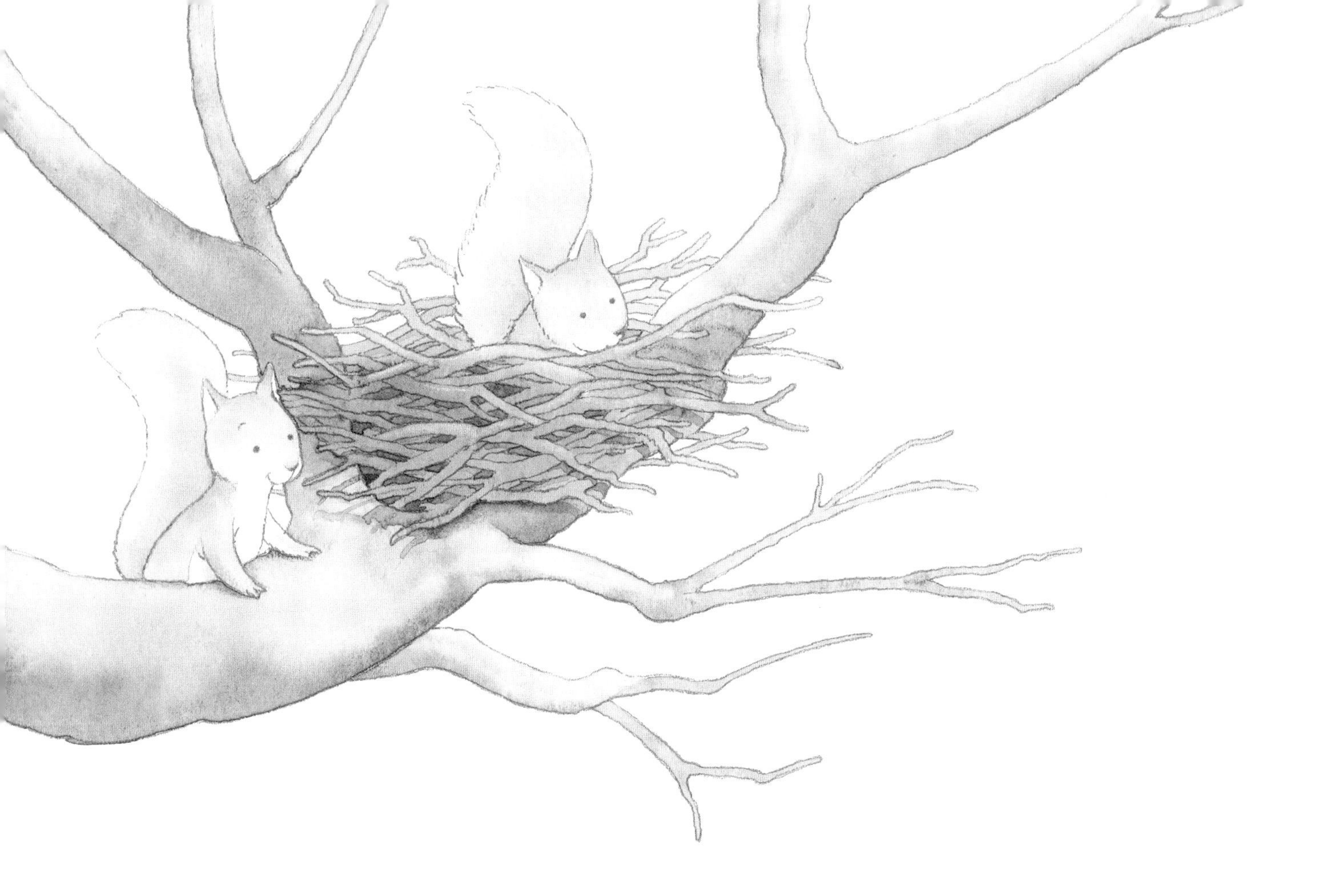

The squirrels had made their nest out of sticks.

'I will build myself a stick nest!' said Kipper. But Kipper's nest was not very good. He could only find…

…three sticks!

The sheep looked very happy
just sitting in the grass.
No, that was no good either.
The grass was much too…

…tickly!

The frog had found a sunny place
in the middle of the pond.
He was sitting on a lily pad.

'I wonder if I could do that,'
said Kipper.

But he couldn't!

'Perhaps a nice dark hole would be good,' thought Kipper. 'The rabbits seem to like them.'

But it was not
a rabbit hole!

Kipper rushed indoors and hid underneath his blanket.

His

lovely

old

smelly

blanket!

Kipper put the blanket back in his basket. He found his rabbit.

'Sorry Rabbit,' he said.

He found his bone and his ball.

'I like my basket just the way it is,' yawned Kipper. He climbed in and pulled the blanket over his head.

'It is the best basket in the whole, wide...

...sssssssssssshh

hhhhhhh!

Kipper's Toybox

Mick Inkpen

Someone or something had been nibbling a hole in Kipper's toybox.

'I hope my toys are safe,' said Kipper. He emptied them out and counted them.

'One, two, three, four, five, six, SEVEN! That's wrong!' he said. 'There should only be six!'

Kipper counted his toys again. This time he lined them up to make it easier.

'Big Owl one, Hippopotamus two, Sock Thing three, Slipper four, Rabbit five, Mr Snake six.

'That's better!' he said.

Kipper put his toys back in the toybox. Then he counted them one more time. Just to make sure.

'One, two, three, four, five, six, seven, EIGHT NOSES! That's two too many noses!' said Kipper.

Kipper grabbed Big Owl and threw him out of the toybox.

'ONE!' he said crossly.

Out went Hippopotamus, 'TWO!'

Out went Rabbit, 'THREE!'

Out went Mr Snake, 'FOUR!'

Out went Slipper, 'FIVE!'

But where was six? Where was Sock Thing?

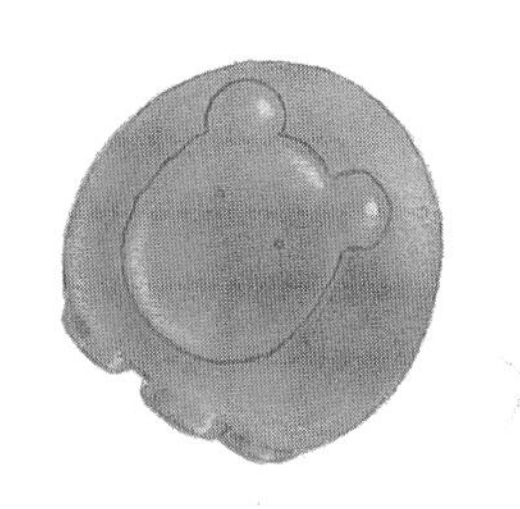

Kipper was upset. Next to Rabbit, Sock Thing was his favourite. Now he was gone.

'I won't lose any more of you,' said Kipper. He picked up the rest of his toys and put them in his basket. Then he climbed in and kept watch until bedtime.

That night Kipper was woken by a strange noise.

It was coming from the corner of the room.

Kipper turned on the light. There, wriggling across the floor, was Sock Thing! It must have been Sock Thing who had been eating his toybox!

Kipper was not sure what to do. None of his toys had ever come to life before. He jumped back in his basket and hid behind Big Owl.

Sock Thing wriggled slowly round in a circle and bumped into the basket. Then he began to wriggle back the way he had come.

He did not seem to know where he was going. Kipper followed.

Quickly Kipper grabbed him by the nose. Sock Thing squeaked and wriggled harder.

Then a little tail appeared. A little pink tail.

And a little voice said, 'Don't hurt him!'

'So it was YOU! You have been making the hole in my toybox!' said Kipper.

It was true. The mice had been nibbling pieces of Kipper's toybox to make their nest.

'You must promise not to nibble it again,' said Kipper.

'We promise,' said the mice.

In return Kipper let the mice share his basket. It was much cosier than a nest made of cardboard and the two little mice never nibbled Kipper's toybox again…

But their babies did.
They nibbled EVERYTHING!

Kipper's Birthday

Mick Inkpen

It was the day before Kipper's birthday. He was busy with his paints making party invitations. In large letters he painted,

Plees come to my bithday party tomoro at 12 o cloc dont be lat

He hung them up to dry and set about making a cake.

Kipper had not made a cake before. He put some currants and eggs and currants and flour and sugar and currants into a bowl. Then he stirred the mixture until his arm ached.

Next he added some cherries and stirred it once more. Then he rolled it with a rolling pin and looked at what he had made.

'I have made a flat thing,' he said.

Kipper squeezed the flat thing into a cake shape and watched it bake in the oven. To his surprise it changed itself slowly into a sort of heap, but it smelled good. He put the last remaining cherry on the top for decoration.

By this time the party invitations were dry.

'I'll deliver them tomorrow,' yawned Kipper. 'It's too late now.'

Kipper woke bright and early on his birthday. His first thought was, 'Balloons! We must have balloons!' But as he rushed downstairs another thought popped into his head. 'Invitations!'

Kipper ran all the way to his best friend's house and stuffed the invitations into Tiger's hand.

'That one's yours! Those are for the others!' he panted. 'Can't stop! Balloons!'

When he had gone Tiger opened the invitation.

Plees come to my bithday party tomoro at 12 o cloc dont be lat

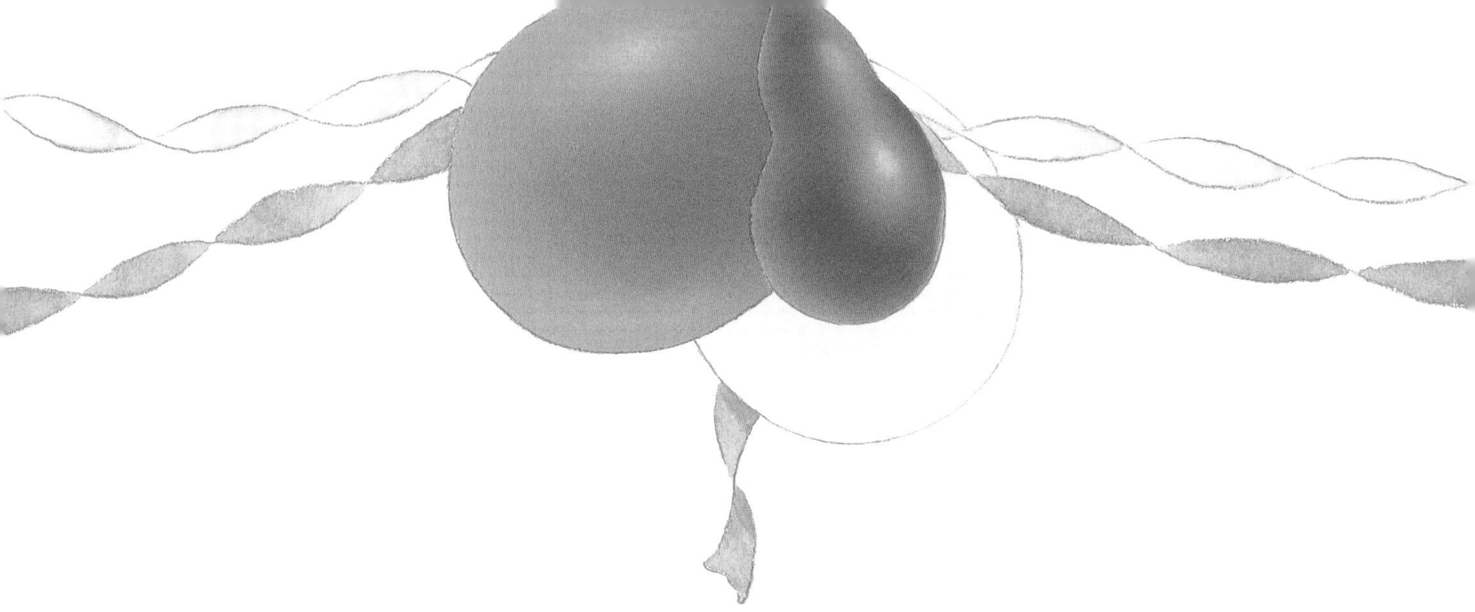

At twelve o'clock Kipper carefully placed his cake on the table and sat down to wait for a knock at the door.

He waited. And he waited. But nobody came. Not even Tiger.

The cake smelled good and Kipper began to feel hungry. At one o'clock he ate the cherry from the top.

Two o'clock passed. Still nobody came. Kipper pulled off a large piece of cake and broke it open to see if there was a cherry inside. There were two. He ate them both and began to feel better.

By five o'clock there were no more cherries to be found.

Kipper stretched out on the table feeling very full and very sleepy.

Kipper slept through the evening and into the night.
He dreamt that he was climbing a mountain made of cake and dodging great cake boulders as they crashed towards him.

Even when the sun streamed through his window the next morning he did not wake, but snored peacefully until noon when he was woken by a knock at the door.

His friends had come.

'Happy birthday, Kipper!' said Jake.

'Happy birthday, Kipper!' said Holly.

'And many happy returns!' said Tiger.

Kipper blinked and rubbed his eyes.

'But my birthday was yesterday,' he said sleepily.

They looked at the invitation.

Plees come to my bithday party
tomoro at 12 o cloc dont be lat

Kipper looked puzzled.

'So my birthday is not until tomorrow,' he said. 'We haven't missed it after all!'

'No, no, no,' said Tiger. 'Your birthday must have been *tomorrow* the day before yesterday.' Kipper looked puzzled again.

Tiger went on, 'So yesterday it would have been *today,* but today it was *yesterday.* Do you see?'

Kipper did not see. His brain was beginning to ache so he said, 'Cake anyone?' And then he remembered that he had eaten it all.

‘Never mind,’ said Tiger. ‘Why don’t you open your presents?’

The presents seemed a bit odd. The first was a napkin from Jake. The second was some candles from Holly.

‘Very useful,’ said Kipper, trying not to look disappointed.

But the third was the most useful of all…

It was a cake!

Kipper's Snowy Day

Mick Inkpen

It was a new morning
and it was snowing!
Huge cotton wool snowflakes were
tumbling past Kipper's window.

'Yes!' said Kipper, jumping out
of his basket. 'Yes! Yes!'

He grabbed his scarf and wound
it three times round his head.
'Yes! Yes! Yes!'

Kipper was very positive
about snow.

Kipper rushed outside. The snow lay deep and smooth and new, like an empty page waiting to be scribbled on. He made a paw print, and then another.

And then with a whoop he went charging round and round, crisscrossing this way and that, until the garden was full of his tracks.

Kipper stopped to catch his breath, letting the swirling snowflakes melt on his tongue. Then he fell backwards into the snow and lay there panting.

When he stood up he found that he had made a perfect Kipper shaped hole. He tried again. Then he tried a different shape. And another.

'I bet Tiger hasn't thought of this,' he said, and ran off to find his best friend.

Kipper found Tiger at the top of Big Hill. He was wrapped up in a fat bundle of silly, woolly clothes. Kipper plopped a friendly snowball on top of his head.

'Hello,' said Tiger.

Tiger pointed up at the sky. A watery sun was seeping through the grey clouds.

'It won't last,' he said. 'It'll all be gone by tomorrow. There's a warm wind coming.' Tiger was like that. He knew things.

But this was not at all what Kipper wanted to hear, so he started throwing snowballs at his friend.

Tiger was very easy to hit because the silly, woolly clothes were wrapped so tightly around him that he could hardly move. And his own snowballs stuck like little pompoms to the silly, woolly gloves.

'Look at my new game,' said Kipper, falling backwards into the snow.

'You get up very carefully… and there you are!' And there he was, or at least the shape of him.

Tiger stretched out his arms, and fell backwards with a soft, woolly 'crump'. But when he tried to get up he could not. He was too round. He just lay there waving his arms and legs like a beetle on its back.

Tiger heaved himself over onto his tummy, but rolled too far, and found himself on his back again. He tried again. The same thing happened. Snow began to stick in thick lumps to the silly, woolly clothes. Crossly, he heaved himself over once more.

This time he rolled over twice, three times, four times…

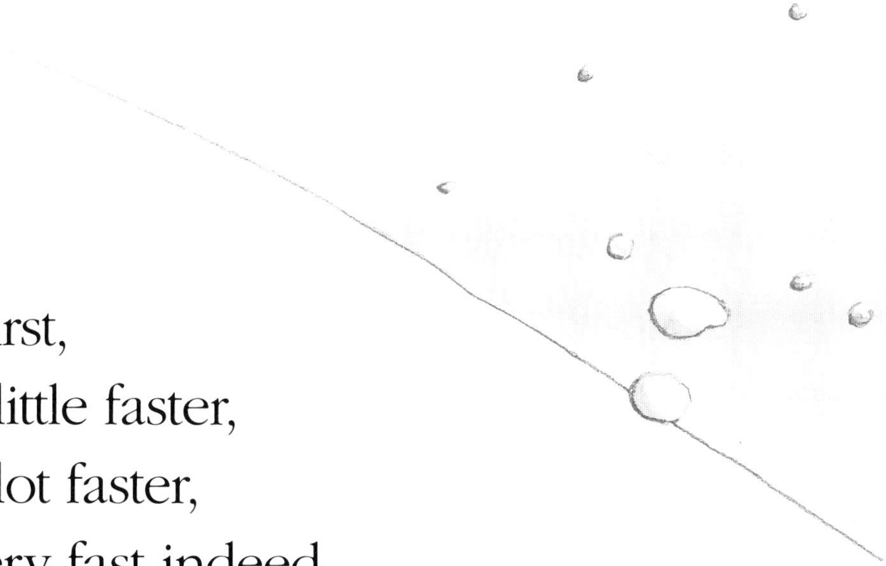

Slowly at first,
and then a little faster,
and then a lot faster,
and then very fast indeed,
he rolled down the hill.

And as he went the silly, woolly clothes picked up more and more snow, so that by the time he reached the bottom he had changed from a small dog into a giant snowball. The giant snowball fell to pieces.

Kipper charged down the hill.

'Are you all right Tiger?' he panted.

Tiger pulled off his silly, woolly hat.

A big grin spread across his face.

'Again!' he said.

So that is what they did, all day long, taking turns to wear the silly, woolly clothes.

And by the time the sun began to dip towards the hill, making their shadows long and skinny, they had rolled enough snow to the bottom to build a giant snowdog.

They watched their shadows lengthen and fade.

'It'll all be gone by tomorrow,' said Tiger. 'There's a warm wind coming.'

But for once Tiger was wrong. The warm wind stayed away, and that night another snowstorm smoothed out all of Kipper's paw prints, making the garden like a clean, white, empty page once more.

And the snowdog stood at the bottom of Big Hill wearing Tiger's silly, woolly clothes...

For almost three…

whole…

weeks.

Other books by Mick Inkpen:

ONE BEAR AT BEDTIME

THE BLUE BALLOON

THREADBEAR

KIPPER'S BOOK OF COUNTING

KIPPER'S BOOK OF COLOURS

KIPPER'S BOOK OF OPPOSITES

KIPPER'S BOOK OF WEATHER

WHERE, OH WHERE, IS KIPPER'S BEAR?

THE LITTLE KIPPERS

THE WIBBLY PIG BOOKS

LULLABYHULLABALLOO!

NOTHING

BILLY'S BEETLE

PENGUIN SMALL

BEAR

British Library Cataloguing in Publication Data

A catalogue record for this book is
available from the British Library

ISBN 0 340 71628 2 (HB)

Kipper first published 1991
Kipper's Toybox first published 1992
Kipper's Birthday first published 1993
Kipper's Snowy Day first published 1996

This edition first published 1998 by
Hodder Children's Books,
A division of Hodder Headline plc,
338 Euston Road, London NW1 3BH

10 9 8 7 6 5 4 3 2 1

Printed in Hong Kong

Goodbye.